COMEBACK OF THE
HOME RUN KID

The #1
Sports Series
for Kids

COMEBACK OF THE
HOME RUN KID

Text by Stephanie Peters

LITTLE, BROWN AND COMPANY

New York ⌁ Boston

To our mother, Cay Christopher, in loving memory

COMEBACK OF THE
HOME RUN KID

1

I've got it! I've got it!"

Sylvester Coddmyer the Third backpedaled from the pitcher's mound. He and his friend Duane Francis were playing a game of pitch, hit, and catch. Duane had just hit a high fly ball toward shortstop. Sylvester was trying to get under it.

"You're going to miss!" Duane called, laughing.

Syl kept moving. If he'd learned one thing from playing on the Hooper Junior High Redbirds baseball team, it was never to give up.

He crossed from the grassy infield to the sandy base path. Head craned back, he searched the sky, found the ball, and realized it was going to fall behind him. Eye still on the ball, he took one more step back.

Suddenly, his left foot wrenched sideways. He gave a sharp cry of pain and fell in a heap. The baseball thudded down next to him and rolled away.

"Syl! Are you all right?" Duane ran up, his face full of concern.

"My ankle!" Syl gasped. "It hurts really bad. I think you better find someone to help me."

Duane scanned the park. His expression went from concern to outright panic. "There's no one around anywhere!"

"My mom's home," Sylvester said. "Can you go get her?"

Duane took off at a dead run in the direction of the Coddmyers' house. Syl lay back on the grass and tried to ignore the pain in his ankle.

"Sylvester!"

A tall blond man wearing a New York Yankees baseball cap and sweats suddenly came into view. Syl blinked in surprise. Hadn't Duane just said there wasn't anyone else in the park?

"That was a bad fall," the man said. He gestured toward Syl's foot. "We should take a look."

Syl hesitated for a moment. But his ankle was really throbbing now and the tightly laced cleat wasn't making it feel any better. So he nodded.

The man carefully took off the cleat and peeled back the sock. He gave a low whistle.

Sylvester sat up and looked at his ankle. It was as puffy as a marshmallow and turning black-and-blue. Suddenly queasy, he lay back down, closed his eyes, and took some deep breaths.

"Is it broken?" he whispered. A broken ankle, he knew, could take a long time to heal. School had just let out — and summer baseball was only a few weeks away. If his ankle was broken, his whole vacation would be ruined!

"I think it's just sprained," the man replied, "but you'll need an X-ray to be sure. For now, we need to get it elevated."

The man grabbed Syl's baseball glove and tucked it underneath the injured ankle. Syl bit his lip, trying not to cry out in pain.

The man sat back on his heels. "It's going to hurt for a while. Even after the swelling goes down and the bruises disappear, that ankle's going to feel pretty weak. You'll have to work hard to strengthen it again. And even then, it might give you some pain."

Syl swallowed hard. "So much for summer

4

baseball." He squeezed his eyes shut but a tear slipped out anyway.

The man was silent. Then he said, "Maybe not. If you want, I could work with you to get you ready to play."

Sylvester's eyes flew open. He stared at the man. Something about this situation — a mysterious man showing up out of nowhere and offering to help him with his game — was eerily familiar.

2

Sylvester Coddmyer the Third's baseball career had started two seasons ago. Back then, he hadn't been a very good player. In fact, he almost didn't make the team that first year.

Then he met a man named George Baruth. With Mr. Baruth's encouragement and advice, his fielding and hitting improved — a lot. To his own and everyone else's amazement, he began making miraculous catches and hitting nothing but homers every time he came up to bat! His home run streak was so remarkable that some people offered to pay him to publish his story in their magazine. But Sylvester turned them down. Money didn't matter to him; he was just happy to be playing the game he loved.

When this past season started, he assumed he'd be just as good a player as he'd been the previous year. Instead, he floundered. His coach, Stan Corbin, had no choice but to bench him. Sylvester spent the first few games watching from the dugout and feeling like a complete loser.

Then a man who called himself Cheeko entered the picture. Sylvester believed that Cheeko was Mr. Baruth's friend. So when Cheeko gave him some pointers to improve his game, Syl listened. Following that advice, Syl started leaning into pitches to get a free trip to first base. He pretended he'd caught fly balls that had really fallen out of his glove. And he "accidentally" bumped into opponents as he rounded the bases.

7

These tricks did help Syl's stats. But it didn't take a rocket scientist to figure out that Cheeko wasn't teaching Sylvester to play better ball. He was teaching him to cheat.

And there was something more, too. Sylvester had a nagging feeling that Cheeko's help went much further than just advice. How else could he explain the weird sensation that he'd gotten an invisible boost in time to make a spectacular top-of-the-fence catch? Or that he'd started getting hits again, and always — *always!* — when there were people on base? Much as he wanted to think that he was doing these things himself, he just couldn't. Somehow, he believed, Cheeko was helping him.

The mystery didn't end there. Toward the end of the season, Sylvester made two startling discoveries.

His friend Duane had a sizable collection of baseball cards. One was of the most famous slugger in the world, George Herman "Babe" Ruth. When Sylvester saw that card, he nearly fainted. The man in the picture looked exactly like Mr. Baruth!

Duane had another card in his collection, this one of southpaw pitcher Eddie Cicotte. Cicotte played for the White Sox in 1919. That year, the White Sox went to the World Series as the heavy favorites to win. Instead, they lost to the underdog Cincinnati Reds, five games to three.

The reason for the surprising defeat soon came to light. Cicotte and seven of his teammates had lost the World Series on purpose! Gamblers had promised to give them a lot of money if they flubbed catches, struck out, and got caught stealing base. Knowing that the White Sox were sure to lose, the gamblers bet on the Reds instead — and made a pile of cash when the Reds won.

People everywhere were outraged when

they learned that the players had thrown the World Series. Dubbed the Black Sox Scandal, it was the biggest disgrace in baseball history. Cicotte and the others were banished from the sport forever. To this day, they are viewed as some of the most dishonest players the game has ever seen.

Sylvester had never heard about Cicotte or the Black Sox Scandal. He was stunned when he saw Cicotte's picture for the first time. The corrupt pitcher was the spitting image of Cheeko!

These discoveries made Syl's imagination go wild. Was it possible that he'd been coached by the ghosts of these two players, one famous, one infamous? It seemed too fantastic to believe, and yet, whenever Sylvester looked at pictures of Cicotte and Babe Ruth, he couldn't help wondering.

But one thing was certain: whether Cheeko was really the disgraced Cicotte or not, Syl no longer trusted him. Right before the last game of the season, he told Cheeko he wasn't going to play dirty anymore. That very afternoon, Cheeko disappeared, never to be seen again. And that very afternoon, Sylvester stopped hammering in hits and, instead, played with the same skill as any other thirteen-year-old kid.

That game had been weeks ago. Now Sylvester stared up at the man in the Yankees cap sitting next to him. Was yet another mystery about to begin — and, if so, how would this one end?

"Who — who are you?" Sylvester asked. "How did you know my name?"

The man smiled. "I'm a ballplayer, like you. And I've recovered from my share of injuries, too. In fact —"

He broke off in mid-sentence. Head cocked to one side, he seemed to be listening to something.

Syl listened, too. He heard car doors slamming shut. He sat up and looked at the parking lot at the far end of the field. There were his mother and Duane!

A wave of relief flooded over him. "It's my mom," he said, turning back to the man.

But the man was no longer there. He had simply vanished!

3

ylvester!" Mrs. Coddmyer hurried to her son's side. "Oh my! How badly does your ankle hurt?"

"Pretty bad," Syl admitted. "But there's something else I —"

His mother cut him off. "I'm calling your doctor." She pulled out her cell phone and punched in the number.

Duane sat down next to him. "Sorry you had to wait out here by yourself."

"But I wasn't alone," Syl said in a low voice. "Didn't you see the man wearing the Yankees cap?"

Duane shook his head. "You were alone when we got here! Maybe you hit your head when you fell — or dreamed up the guy?"

Sylvester sank back onto the grass. His ankle was throbbing worse than ever. "Maybe I did," he murmured.

His mother clicked her cell phone shut. "The doctor says to go right to the emergency room for X-rays. Duane, can you help me get him to the car?"

The rest of the day passed in a blur. The X-ray of the ankle showed it wasn't broken. But the doctor told Syl to stay off it for a week or so.

"Rest, ice, and elevate that ankle every day," she said as she pushed her patient in a wheelchair out to the car. "Start doing those exercises I showed you in a few days. And before you play any more baseball, get yourself a sturdy ankle brace. You don't want to suffer a reinjury!"

It wasn't until that night, after Sylvester had finally crawled into bed, that he thought about his meeting with the mysterious man in the Yankees cap. He toyed with the idea of searching for information on him. He was pretty sure he knew where to look: baseball books, websites of old-time ball players, and Duane's baseball card collection.

But in the end, he decided against it. While part of him was burning with curiosity, a bigger part of him wanted to see what would happen next. Would the man reappear and help him with his game, as he had said he would? And if he did, would he be like Cheeko or Mr. Baruth?

But as the days went by, the man didn't show up. By the middle of the next week, Sylvester had almost convinced himself that Duane had been right. He had dreamed up the man after all.

✤   ✤   ✤

"Checkmate! I win again!" Duane knocked over Sylvester's black king with his own white bishop and smiled triumphantly. Then his smile faded.

"You could at least *look* like you cared that you just lost for the fifth time in a row!" Duane grumbled as he gathered up the chess pieces.

Sylvester blinked. The day's weather was perfect for baseball. But instead of throwing, catching, and batting, Syl was sitting inside, his ankle elevated on an ottoman.

He blew out his breath in frustration. "Sorry, Duane," he replied. "I guess I'm getting bored of these board games."

"Oh." Duane gave a small laugh. "For a moment there, I thought you were getting bored of me!" He finished putting the pieces back in the box and closed the lid. "Say, you hear anything from Joyce?"

Joyce Dancer was Syl's other close friend. She was away for the summer, vacationing on Cape Cod with her family.

"I got an e-mail the other day. She sounds like she's having fun."

"Did you tell her about your ankle?"

Syl shrugged. "What's to tell? I sprained it, and now I'm sitting around all day waiting for it to get better instead of playing ball like I want to!"

In another room, the phone rang. Sylvester heard his mother answer it. A few minutes later, she came into the room carrying a tray with a pitcher of lemonade, some glasses, and a bowl of popcorn on it.

As Mrs. Coddmyer served the lemonade, she said, "That was Coach Corbin on the phone. He was calling to let you know that you'll be on his team, the Hooper Hawks. First practice is the day after tomorrow."

She smiled at Duane. "When he found out you were here, he told me to let you know you're a Hawk, too."

"Yes!" Duane pumped his fist.

Sylvester sat back, his mind in a whirl. Stan Corbin was a great coach and Sylvester was psyched to have been chosen for his Hawks. But he was also nervous. He'd been the best player on the team for two seasons, so the coach had to be expecting fantastic things from him. But he hadn't picked up a bat, ball, or glove since the accident. What if he couldn't perform up to the coach's expectations? And what would his ankle feel like when he finally did get back on the field?

Sylvester didn't want to disappoint Coach Corbin by playing poorly. But he was afraid that's just what was going to happen.

Just then, the phone rang again. Mrs. Coddmyer hurried to answer it.

Duane raised his lemonade glass. "To the

future baseball champs, the Hooper Hawks!"
He clinked his glass against Sylvester's and
took a big gulp.

Sylvester tried to match Duane's happy
mood. But the lemonade tasted sour to him
and he couldn't help but make a face.

"What's wrong?" Duane asked.

Sylvester gestured at his ankle. "Three
guesses!"

Duane waved his concern away. "It'll be
fine by the first practice!"

Sylvester shook his head. "Yeah, but even
if it is, I haven't played ball for weeks —"

"It hasn't even been two!" Duane interrupted.

"So what if I'm no good when I finally can
play again?"

Duane tossed some popcorn in his mouth
and chewed thoughtfully. "When are you supposed to start doing stuff again?"

"The doctor said tomorrow."

Duane grinned broadly. "So we meet at the diamond for some pitch, hit, and catch tomorrow morning and test it. Deal?"

Duane's enthusiasm was infectious and Sylvester couldn't help but grin back. "Okay, you got a deal!" he said. He picked up his lemonade and took a huge swallow. This time, the cold drink tasted sweet and delicious.

4

The next morning after breakfast, Sylvester put on his new ankle brace and called Duane to say he was ready to play.

"Awesome!" Duane replied. "I'll get my glove, bat, and ball and meet you at the field in twenty minutes, okay?"

"I'll bring my bat, too. See you there!"

Duane was already on the diamond when Syl arrived. "Bad news!" he called when he saw Sylvester. "I can only stay for half an hour. I've got to go to the dentist." He made a disgusted face. "Other kids get to be late to school because of dentist appointments. But my mom has to schedule one during summer vacation! Sheesh!"

Sylvester was only a little disappointed, however. Even with the brace, his ankle felt a bit weak and wobbly after the walk to the park. It was aching a little, too. He thought he might be ready to rest it after half an hour anyway.

"So what do you want to do first, pitch or hit?" Duane asked him.

"How about we warm up with a game of catch?" Syl countered.

"You got it!"

As Duane jogged farther into the field, Sylvester thought — not for the first time — how lucky he was to have such a good buddy. Duane was an easygoing kid. He liked sports, but he wasn't super-competitive about them. He hardly ever got down on himself when he was playing poorly, he didn't boast when he made a great play, and he never yelled at anyone who flubbed up. He'd stuck by Syl through thick and thin the last two baseball seasons, no matter how Syl had been performing. Syl hoped Duane knew how much that meant to him.

"Heads up!" Duane called. He lobbed the ball high into the clear blue sky.

When the ball came down, it landed with a satisfying *plop* in the pocket of Syl's glove. Syl palmed it, hollered "Incoming!," and threw with all his might.

The ball zipped straight for Duane's outstretched glove. It struck hard enough for Syl to hear the *pop* it made against the leather.

"Yow!" Duane cried. He took his hand out of his glove and shook it. "Nothing wrong with your arm! That one stung!" He hurled the ball back to Syl.

The two boys played catch for ten minutes. Then Duane suggested that he pitch some to Syl. "But you have to promise not to clobber them. I don't feel like running all the way to the fence and back after every hit!"

"For you," Syl replied with a grin, "I'll keep it in the infield!" He picked up his bat and took a few easy practice swings.

Man, he thought as he listened to the bat hum through the air, *it's good to hold one of these again!*

He took up his stance. He was a righty, so he stood to the left of the plate with his left leg forward, the bat above his right shoulder.

When Syl was ready, Duane fired a pitch toward the plate.

The moment he saw Duane let loose, Syl began his swing. He lifted his left foot a few inches off the ground and rotated his upper body backward to move the bat farther behind him. Then he planted his left foot on the ground, twisted his hips and shoulders toward the mound, and brought the bat around. The whole motion was automatic and took only seconds.

Then, as the bat reached the spot where it would meet the ball, he straightened his front leg — and felt a sharp stab of pain in his left ankle.

"Ow!" He whiffed the pitch, dropped the bat, and clutched his ankle.

Duane hurried over, looking anxious. "What happened?"

But Sylvester couldn't answer because his throat was suddenly tight with tears. Instead, he dipped his head, removed his brace, and rubbed his ankle until the pain subsided.

"Guess I'm still not one hundred percent," he said finally, his voice thick with dismay.

"So you're not ready to hit just yet," Duane said. "You can still throw and catch, right?" He checked his watch. "I've got about ten minutes before I'm supposed to be home. Want to toss it back and forth some more?"

But Sylvester no longer felt like playing catch. He stood up, using the bat like a crutch. "I dunno, Duane. I think I'll head home, put ice on my ankle for a while."

A shadow of disappointment crossed Duane's face. But he didn't protest. "Okay, Syl. Want me to come over after my dentist appointment? We can play another board game or something."

Syl just shrugged and looked away.

After a moment, Duane stuck his glove on the fat end of his bat. "Well, see you around, I guess." He retrieved his baseball, shouldered the bat, and walked off the field.

Syl watched him go. Then he swung his bat at a small stone. "Rats," he murmured as the pebble bounced into the grass. He put the brace back on, picked up his glove, and set off for home.

5

Sylvester hadn't gone more than a block when he heard someone call his name.

"Syl! Sylvester Coddmyer the Third!"

He turned around and saw a big blond man in a baseball cap, sweatshirt, and sweat pants jogging toward him. Sylvester's eyes widened when he saw the cap had a New York Yankees insignia above the brim.

"You're the guy who helped me after I hurt my ankle!" he cried in astonishment. "I thought I'd dreamed you up!"

The man laughed. "Better a dream than a

nightmare! How've you been, pal?" He took a step toward Syl.

As the man loomed closer, Syl had a sudden thought. Maybe he hadn't dreamed up this guy — but that didn't mean the man was okay. He was a stranger.

"Um, I think I'd better be going, mister," he said, edging away.

The man blinked. Then a look of understanding crossed his face. "Syl," he said quietly. "I'm not going to hurt you. In fact, I want to help you."

Syl continued to back away. "Thanks anyway, but I don't need any help."

The man took off his cap and scratched his head. "I understand your caution. Being wary of strangers is smart." He put his cap back on. "Tell you what. I'm going to head over to the baseball diamond. If you change your mind, you can find me there."

He started to walk away. Then he turned

back. "By the way, the pain you're having in your ankle when you swing? I have an idea that might help."

Syl's jaw dropped. "How did you know about that?"

The man shrugged. "Lucky guess."

Sylvester watched him go. As he did, he thought about Mr. Baruth and Cheeko. Both of those men had been strangers, too. And both had given him pointers that had improved his game. Sure, Cheeko's tips hadn't been on the up-and-up, but he wouldn't have traded Mr. Baruth's advice for the world.

"I wish he were here right now," Syl said out loud. "He'd know if it was okay to go with that guy or not."

"With what guy?"

Syl whirled around and came face-to-face with a skinny kid with glasses.

"Snooky!" he cried. "Man, don't sneak up on me like that!"

It was Snooky Malone. Snooky was a nice enough kid, if a little weird. He believed in astrology and was interested in anything to do with the paranormal. Ghosts, extrasensory perception, mythical beings — those were the things Snooky liked. He often tracked Sylvester down to tell him the latest predictions he'd gleaned from reading Sylvester's star charts and horoscopes. Syl had to admit that sometimes Snooky's predictions were pretty accurate. Snooky liked baseball, too, so Syl usually didn't mind hanging out with him.

"Sorry, Syl. I thought you heard me come up," Snooky said now. "Why are you standing here talking to yourself?"

Sylvester reddened. "I, uh, I was just thinking out loud. Listen, I gotta go. See ya, Snooky."

"Wait! I have something to show you!" He pulled a piece of newspaper out of his pocket and cleared his throat.

Sylvester groaned. "Snooky, how many times do I have to tell you that I'm not interested in hearing my horoscope?"

Snooky looked offended. "I'm not here to tell you about that, although now that you mention it, today's reading did say something about a comet entering your —"

Syl groaned again.

"Okay, okay." Snooky grumbled. "Forget the horoscope. But you *might* want to hear this!" He adjusted his glasses, consulted the paper, and began to read.

"Teams for this summer's fourteen-and-under baseball league were announced this week. There will be six squads in all, made up of players from the nearby towns of Hooper, Lansing, Macon, and Broton. The teams will be called —"

Snooky broke off. "Okay, that's not the interesting part. Hold on, hold on." He scanned the article. "Wait, here it is!

"*This reporter spoke with the coach for the Hooper Hawks, Stan Corbin. Coach Corbin expressed his enthusiasm for the coming season, adding, 'I'm especially looking forward to seeing how the star of my last team, Sylvester Coddmyer the Third, will perform this time around.' Coddmyer, readers may remember, astounded baseball fans two years ago with —* hey, Syl! Where are you going?"*

But Syl didn't answer. He'd stopped listening once he'd heard the quote from Coach Corbin. Now he was hurrying back to the ballpark as fast as his sore ankle would take him, hoping that the big blond man would still be there.

I knew it, Syl thought anxiously. *The coach is counting on me to be his number one player again this year! I've got to get all the help I can.*

He spotted the man with the Yankees cap sitting on the bench beside the baseball diamond. Near him was a bucket filled with baseballs.

Syl didn't approach him right away, however. Instead, he ducked behind a tree and looked around the park. In the distance he saw a group of kids starting a game of kickball. In another section two girls were tossing a Frisbee back and forth. The playground was swarming with preschoolers busy climbing, swinging, and sliding while their mothers watched over them and chatted with one another.

Seeing so many people around, including several adults, made Syl feel safe. He came out from behind the tree.

"Hey, mister?"

The man waved. "Syl! I take it you changed your mind?"

Sylvester joined him on the bench. "Yeah, but can I ask you something first?"

"Ask away."

"Do you know Mr. George Baruth?"

The man looked surprised. "George Baruth? I've heard of him. But have I ever met him? No. And I can tell you right now, he's never heard of me." Then he smiled. "But I think we'd be friends if we ever did meet. We've got a lot in common."

Syl thought about the man's answer. He knew he'd feel better if the blond man had said he was Mr. Baruth's friend. But he guessed he had to appreciate the fact that he hadn't lied to him about it, the way Cheeko had.

"Anything else, Syl?"

"Um, just one other thing," Sylvester replied. "What's your name?"

Now the man laughed. "How about you call me Charlie Comet?"

Syl blinked. "Charlie . . . Comet?" *Hadn't Snooky said his horoscope mentioned a comet? Weird!*

"Way back when some people used to call me the Comet," the man explained.

Sylvester wanted to ask why but didn't get the chance because Charlie tossed a ball from the bucket to him.

"We could stand here and talk about nicknames all day," Charlie said. "But personally, I'd rather be playing ball. Wouldn't you?"

Sylvester gestured toward his ankle. "You said you had an idea that might keep my ankle from hurting?"

Charlie brightened. "I thought you'd never ask!" He picked up a bat and crossed to home plate. "Throw me a few pitches, will you?"

Sylvester put on his glove and walked to the mound. Charlie took up a right-handed stance. Sylvester hurled the ball with as much speed and accuracy as he could muster.

The ball zipped toward the plate. Charlie swung. *Crack!* It was a hard grounder right back at the mound. Sylvester crouched and scooped up the ball with his glove.

"Good," Charlie said. "Now send that pill my way again!"

Once more Syl threw. This time, Charlie connected down low and lofted the ball high into the sky. Sylvester took a few steps back and got under it. But when the ball came down, it bounced off the tip of his glove and fell behind him.

"Rats!" Sylvester said. He retrieved the ball and turned to face Charlie again. His eyes widened with surprise.

Charlie was in his batting stance. But this time, instead of hitting righty, he was in position to bat lefty!

7

Sylvester hesitated, wondering if Charlie had made a mistake. But Charlie motioned for him to throw. So Syl did — and Charlie walloped the ball far into the outfield.

"Wow! Great hit!" Syl yelled, twisting around to see where the ball landed.

Charlie grinned broadly. "Thank you kindly! Think you could do that, too?"

"I don't know," Sylvester admitted. "I've hit plenty of homers, but —"

Charlie's laugh interrupted him. "I wasn't talking about the hit, Syl." He carried the bucket of balls to the pitcher's mound. "What I meant was, do you think you could bat lefty?"

Sylvester gaped. "Bat *lefty*?" he echoed. "But I'm right-handed!"

"So am I!" Charlie's eyes twinkled. "When I was a young boy, my dad taught me how to switch-hit. He practiced with me for hours until hitting both righty and lefty felt natural."

"But why would it matter?" Syl asked. "I mean, looks to me like you can hit really well from the right."

"True. But a strong switch-hitter can be good for a team. Lefties hit better against right-handed pitchers, and vice versa. If you're a switch-hitter, it doesn't matter who's on the mound, because you can hit a south-paw or a righty equally well."

"I never thought about that," Syl said.

"Well, my dad did," Charlie said. "He

believed I had a talent for baseball and thought if I could switch-hit I'd go farther than if I just hit righty."

"And did you?"

A ghost of a smile crossed Charlie's face. "I went far enough." He held out the bat to Sylvester. "So want to give it a try?"

Sylvester didn't take the bat right away. "I don't know, Charlie. I'm already having problems batting righty. I doubt I'll be any better from the other side."

"Won't know until you give it a go," Charlie quipped. "Come on. I've got a good feeling about this."

So Syl took the bat, walked to the batter's box to the right of home plate, and got into a stance. It felt strange to hold the bat above his left shoulder instead of his right and to turn the right side of his body toward the mound instead of his left.

Charlie chose a ball from the bucket. "Ready?" he called.

Sylvester nodded.

"Then here comes one, nice and easy." Charlie threw. The ball seemed to float toward home plate. Syl swung — and missed completely.

"Well, that stunk!" he grumbled.

Charlie laughed. "Hey, it's only your first try! Take some slow-motion practice swings to get the feel for it."

Syl took up a lefty stance again and swung the bat as if to meet an incoming pitch. As he lifted his right foot off the ground to step into the swing, he felt a slight twinge in his left ankle. But it was nothing compared to the pain he'd felt when he'd batted against Duane earlier, so he ignored it.

After he'd swung half a dozen times, he picked up the ball he'd missed, planning to throw it back to Charlie. But instead, he tossed it high above his head and tried to hit it.

Thock! He sent the small white sphere bouncing through the grassy infield between first and second.

"I did it!" Sylvester cried in astonishment.

Charlie applauded by thumping his bare hand against his glove. "Well done! Now let's see you hit a pitch!" He grabbed a ball from the bucket.

Syl returned to the right side of the batter's box. *I'm going to really clock that ball this time!* he thought gleefully.

But when the ball came, he whiffed. On the next pitch, he managed to connect but only for a little dribbler that stopped a few feet from the plate. He missed the next three pitches, tapped a foul ball down the first baseline on the fourth, and then lost track of the number of times he hit nothing but air. Soon the ground behind Sylvester was littered with baseballs — and Sylvester's mood had gone from excited to disappointed to downright black.

"I can't do it," he mumbled when Charlie approached with the empty bucket. "I might as well just give up now."

Charlie raised his eyebrows but didn't say anything. Instead, he began filling the bucket. Sylvester sighed and reached for the nearest ball.

"Got a question for you," Charlie said suddenly. "How's your ankle feel?"

Sylvester straightened. "It doesn't feel so bad!" he replied with dawning amazement. "A little sore, but . . ."

He sat down, took off the ankle brace, and rubbed at the dull ache. Then he looked up at Charlie. "Is it because I've been batting lefty?"

Charlie nodded. "Think about the mechanics of the right-handed swing," he said. He hefted a bat and got into a righty stance. Moving in slow motion, he lifted his front foot — his left foot — a few inches and moved the bat backward. Then he stepped down and swung, extending and straightening his front leg. The heel of his back foot lifted as he pivoted up onto his toes.

But by that point, his left foot bore most of his weight. And as the bat traveled past the front of his body, the inside edge of that foot lifted up. Just a fraction of an inch, but that was enough to roll the ankle outward. Charlie froze in that position and glanced at Syl.

Syl stared at the foot. "The way your ankle is twisted is just how I hurt mine two weeks ago! That's why you want me to bat lefty — so my injured ankle won't twist outward and get hurt again!"

8

Sylvester was excited. His ankle wasn't going to keep him from playing summer baseball after all! All he had to do was learn to bat lefty!

Thump! The sound of a baseball landing in the bucket brought him back to reality. He looked at the balls in the dirt near the backstop. His excitement faded once more.

All I have to do is learn to bat lefty! he mocked himself. *Like I'll be able to do that in time for the start of the season!*

Charlie picked up on Syl's change of mood instantly. "Sylvester," he said. "You can't expect to become a switch-hitter after just one practice. It's going to take some time and a lot of hard work on your part."

Syl picked up a ball and tossed it from one hand to the other. "But what if I can't do it?"

Charlie gave him a warm smile. "I wouldn't be here if I didn't think you could. So if you're willing to give it your all, I'm willing to give you my time."

Slowly, Sylvester's good mood returned. "Okay," he said. "I'm in."

"Great!" Charlie replied. "Let's get back to work."

For the next hour, Charlie pitched ball after ball to Sylvester. Each time Syl made contact, Charlie gave him the thumbs-up sign. When Syl missed — which happened much more often — Charlie offered words of advice.

"Think about moving your hands toward your back shoulder when you bring the bat back," he called. "That will put the bat in the better position for a strong swing."

"Use your whole body when you swing!" he yelled when Syl flailed at the ball. "Remember, rotating your shoulders and your hips around gives you power!"

When Syl chopped at a pitch, Charlie came off the mound and grabbed his left arm. "You've got to loosen up," he chided, waggling the limb around like it was made of rubber. "If that arm is all shrugged up and tight, it's going to be useless."

The sun was high overhead when Sylvester asked if they could call it quits. "My ankle's feeling a little sore," he admitted. His stomach gave a loud growl. "Guess I'm hungry, too."

Charlie laughed. "Okay. But feel free to take home the baseballs. I won't be using them, but maybe you can."

Syl headed toward shortstop to pick up a ball he'd managed to hit there. "I know it's only my first day trying to hit lefty," he said as he bent down. "But I think I'm starting to get the hang of it. What do you think?"

There was no reply. He straightened.

"Charlie?"

But Charlie was gone.

Syl gripped the ball in his hand tightly. *Just like the day I hurt my ankle*, he thought. *One minute he's here, the next he's vanished into thin air. Just like a —*

"Well, well, well, look who's here!"

Sylvester whirled around. Striding toward him with a bat and a glove was his old enemy, Duke Farrell. The last time Syl saw him, Duke was pitching for the Macon Falcons against the Hooper Redbirds. Sylvester crushed a three-run homer off of him that game, something he was sure Duke hadn't forgotten — or, it was clear, forgiven. With Duke was another Falcon, Steve Button.

"What are you doing here, Syl-ves-ter

Codd-*fish*?" Duke snarled. "Playing a little game of one-on-*none* with your bucket of mangy old baseballs?"

Steve guffawed.

"Oh, go soak your heads!" Sylvester threw his ball into the bucket and reached for the bucket's handle.

Duke's foot lashed out and knocked the bucket over, spilling the balls into the grass. Steve laughed again. Duke didn't even smile. He stared at Syl, his eyes narrowed with an unspoken challenge.

"I heard you like to take cheap shots at other players, Codd-*fish*." Duke's voice was full of menace. "Heard it from a kid on my new team, the Grizzlies. His name is Russ Skelton. Maybe you remember him."

Sylvester froze. He remembered Russ Skelton, all right. Russ had played shortstop for the Lansing Wildcats last season. He'd taunted Syl one game, saying Syl had only gotten a hit because the pitcher had thrown him a "meatball." The comment had made Syl angry. So, taking Cheeko's advice, he'd delivered a hard jab to Russ's ribs as he'd rounded the bases.

Looking back, Syl knew that, like everything else Cheeko had taught him, the jab had been wrong. Thinking about it now made his face turn beet red with shame.

"Yeah, Skelton was sore for days after that game," Duke was saying. "And there's something else, too. A friend of mine videotaped that game. When we watched it, we saw something very interesting." Duke stuck his nose in Syl's face. "That great catch you made? Didn't really happen! The video showed the ball touching the ground!"

Once again, Syl knew exactly what Duke was talking about. Toward the end of the game, he had hurled himself across the grass, glove outstretched, to catch a fly ball. And he had caught it — almost. In truth, the ball had wobbled out of his glove. But when the umpire had called it an out, Syl hadn't corrected him.

Duke took a step closer to Syl, tapping the fat part of the bat in his hand. "I don't think that sort of dirty play should go unpunished. What do you think, Codd-*fish*?"

9

Heads up!" Out of nowhere, a baseball flew across the field and struck Duke square in the back.

"Ow!" Duke dropped his bat, clutched his back with both hands, and let out a string of angry words.

"Whoops, my bad!" a new voice said innocently.

It was Duane. Behind him were Jim Cowley, second baseman for the Redbirds, and Trent Sturgis, shortstop and powerhouse hitter for the same team. Sylvester had had some problems with Trent early last season, but the two had mended fences and become friends. Syl was very happy to see him — and Duane and Jim — now.

Duke and Steve were not. "I'll get you for that," Duke growled at Duane. Then he wheeled around and gave Sylvester a long stare. "And you better hope you're sick the day my Grizzlies play your stupid Hawks."

With that last threat, he grabbed his bat and stalked away with Steve at his heels.

Sylvester blew out a long breath of relief. "Man, am I glad you all came along when you did!" he said to Trent, Jim, and Duane.

Trent waved his hand. "Aww, those guys are so full of hot air that when you poke 'em, they fly around backward!"

The other boys broke up laughing.

"What are you doing here anyway, Syl?" Duane asked. "I thought you were heading home."

He looked from Syl to the pile of spilled

baseballs in the grass and back to Syl. His smile faded. "But I guess you found someone else to play with, huh?"

Sylvester was suddenly tongue-tied. Part of him wanted to tell Duane everything about the mysterious Charlie Comet. After all, he'd told him about Cheeko and Mr. Baruth when he'd seen Duane's baseball cards.

But something stopped him now. Duane had never met Cheeko or Mr. Baruth. Maybe if he had, he would have understood Sylvester's amazement over their resemblances to Cicotte and the Babe. Instead, Duane had shrugged them off as look-alikes. And he thought Syl had dreamed up Charlie. If Syl said he'd just been playing baseball with him, Duane would think he was crazy!

And what would Trent and Jim think about Syl's special coaches or the fact that this new one was teaching him to switch-hit? He wasn't sure he wanted any of them to know about that — at least, not until he was confident he could do it.

So instead of answering Duane, Syl made a big show of looking at his watch. "Man, is that the time?"

He collected the baseballs as if he were in a huge hurry. Jim and Trent lent a hand. After a moment, Duane did, too.

"Funny," Duane said, "I don't remember you bringing this bucket to the field earlier."

"Oh, these are just some practice balls," Syl mumbled evasively. "Anyway, I'll see you guys later." He picked up the bucket and hurried away.

"Hey!" Duane shouted after him. "You missed one!"

"Keep it!" Syl shouted back.

When he reached his house, he stowed his gear in the garage and headed into the kitchen to make some lunch. Only when he was sitting at the table with his sandwich did he let his mind wander over everything that had happened that day. As he did, very different feelings rose to the surface.

He was nervous and excited about batting lefty. Nervous, because he had no idea if he'd be able to do it. Excited, because if he mastered that skill, he might — just might — be the kind of player Coach Corbin expected him to be.

But another emotion was bubbling inside him, too: guilt. It had struck him like a blow when Duke accused him of hitting Russ and faking the catch — and it had grown since then as Syl remembered all the other cheap and dirty tricks he'd played last season.

Coach Corbin thinks I'm a good player, Syl thought, *but only because he doesn't know what I was up to then. If he finds out . . .*

His sandwich suddenly tasted like paste in his mouth. He swallowed hard, pushed the plate away, and put his head down on the table.

If he finds out, he'll know I'm a cheater and bench me for sure. Or worse, kick me off the team! Unless . . .

Sylvester sat up again. *Unless I'm so valuable that he can't afford to bench me!*

With that thought in mind, he sucked down some juice, finished his sandwich, and retrieved the bucket of balls from the garage. He spent the remainder of the afternoon in his backyard, tossing baseballs into the air and trying to hit them left-handed.

By dinnertime, he thought he'd improved a little. But he knew he had a lot more practicing ahead of him before he'd be ready to try batting lefty in a game. He went to bed that night wondering when he'd see Charlie Comet again.

He wondered, too, just who Charlie was and why he had chosen to help Sylvester.

10

The next morning, Syl decided not to worry about Charlie, Duke, or his switch-hitting and to concentrate instead on the Hawks' first practice.

Syl's mother dropped him off at the field with a reminder that she would pick him up when practice was through. "You've got to get a haircut," she told him. "And don't forget to wear your ankle brace, okay?"

Syl nodded and joined the other players on the field. He knew most of them, at least by sight. When he spotted Duane he hurried to his side.

"Hey, Duane, did you guys have a good time at the park after I left?"

Duane gave him a long look. "Yeah," he said finally.

"Oh," said Syl, a little surprised at the coolness in Duane's usually warm voice. "Um, did you play pitch, hit, and catch, or —"

"Coach Corbin is calling you," Duane interrupted. "'Scuse me." He moved away.

"Hey, Sylvester, good to have you on the team," Coach Corbin boomed. "Heard about your ankle injury. Not going to give you any trouble today, is it?"

"It's feeling fine, coach," Syl replied.

"Good. Go join the others, then."

Sylvester did as he was told.

"Welcome, Hawks!" Coach Corbin said. "Today's practice will be simple. We'll warm up. Then I'll split you into two squads for a scrimmage. When it's your turn in the field, go to your favorite position. If two players want the same spot, work it out as best you can. I'll be watching each of you to see what your strengths are. And I know we have some strong players!"

He gave Syl a smile. Syl reddened.

Ten minutes later, warm-up exercises were done and the team was divided into two. Sylvester was disappointed that he and Duane were on opposite sides. He'd hoped to talk to his friend, find out what was bothering him.

Oh well, guess I'll ask him later, he thought as he jogged out to center field. No one else seemed interested in that position, so he got ready for the first batter, crouching low and pounding his fist into his glove.

Up at the plate was a tall boy named A. C. Compton. A. C. had played for the Lansing Wildcats last season. He hadn't been much of a hitter then. But he must have been practicing, for he slugged the first pitch Rick Wilson — former hurler for the Redbirds — threw over the plate. The ball rocketed toward left. The outfielder ran for it and caught it backhanded on the second bounce. A. C. was safe at first, so the left fielder threw the ball back to Rick.

"Nice pickup, Kirk!" Coach Corbin called.

Syl looked at the left fielder again. It was Kirk Anderson of the Macon Falcons — Duke's old team. Syl wondered uneasily if Kirk was friends with Duke — and if so, if he knew what Duke knew about his cheating last season.

Next up was Duane. He took two strikes, a ball, and then, on the fourth pitch, struck out. Shoulders sagging, he walked back to the bench.

"Next time, Duane!" the coach said. "Two more outs, people, then we'll switch sides."

But those two outs were a long time coming. After striking out Duane, Rick couldn't seem to find the plate. He walked one batter and hit the next on the shoulder. Now there were runners on first and second.

Coach Corbin trotted out to the mound to have a few quiet words with the pitcher. Rick nodded vigorously and the coach returned to the sidelines.

"Let's see your stuff, Rick!" he called.

Rick fired in a blazing fastball that stuck in the catcher's glove with a solid *whomp!* The catcher, the batter, and even Rick looked surprised. Then Rick's face lit up with a delighted grin. That strike seemed to give him the boost he needed. He struck out the next two batters to retire the side.

"Way to go!" Syl cried.

He jogged in from the outfield, passing Duane, who was on his way to third base. Sylvester tried to catch his friend's eye, but Duane just pushed by him.

"Up at bat is Trent Sturgis, Kirk Anderson, then Leon Hollister!" Coach Corbin announced. "Okay, Burk, whenever you're ready!"

Pitcher Burk Riley and his brother, Bus, had both played for the Seneca Indians last spring. Now Burk was on the mound for the Hawks and Bus was at shortstop.

Burk caught the throw from catcher Eddie Exton. Trent stepped into the batter's box and hefted the bat into position. Burk reared back and threw.

Zip! The ball buzzed past Trent and landed with a *smack* in Eddie's glove.

"Strike one!" the coach called.

Burk nodded with satisfaction. Trent dug his left toe into the dirt and twirled the bat in small circles above his shoulder. He looked like a tightly wound spring ready to uncoil at the slightest touch.

Burk's next pitch made a beeline toward

the plate. *Crack!* Trent sent the ball right back at him.

"Aahh!" Burk ducked. The ball flew over him, hit the dirt near second base, and took a crazy hop into the outfield. By the time the center fielder got hold of it, Trent was dusting off his pants at first.

"All right, Trent!" Syl called. Then he bent down to remove his brace. His ankle was itching like crazy, and he wanted to give it a good scratch.

Pow! Kirk Anderson singled down the third baseline and sprinted to first. Trent made it safely to second.

Leon Hollister, formerly of the Wildcats, selected a bat, strode confidently to the plate, and stared at Burk. Burk stared back and then whipped in a pitch. Leon lambasted the ball just to the right of second. He, Trent, and Kirk all took off running.

The second baseman scrambled for the

ball and turned to throw Kirk out at second. But Bus, the shortstop, had forgotten to cover the bag. The second baseman switched direction in mid-throw and sent the ball toward first instead.

The throw was wild and — *bam!* — the ball nailed Leon right in the head! Leon dropped like a ton of bricks. Coach Corbin rushed to his side. Some of the players moved to help, but the coach waved them off. Burk ran up to his brother and started to chew him out. Bus thumped his glove against his leg, obviously upset with himself. Kirk, Trent, and Duane huddled near third, talking in low tones.

A few minutes later, Leon got to his feet, supported by the coach. Syl and the others clapped their encouragement.

"Man, if it hadn't been for that batter's helmet, I bet he'd be out cold!" a player beside Syl commented.

Sylvester was only half-listening. The rest of his attention was on third base. Duane, Kirk, and Trent were still deep in conversation.

Wonder what they're talking about? Syl thought.

At that moment, Kirk caught Syl looking at them. He said something to the others. Duane and Trent glanced at Sylvester and then quickly turned their backs.

That's when Syl figured out that they were talking about him. And he had a good idea of what the topic was. *Duke must have told Kirk about my cheating! And now Kirk is telling Duane and Trent!*

11

"**C**oddmyer, are you deaf? The coach just said you're up!"

Sylvester blinked. He'd been so focused on Duane, Kirk, and Trent that he hadn't heard the coach call his name. Now he grabbed a bat and headed to home plate.

Burk's first pitch was low and inside. Sylvester let it go by for a called strike. The next pitch hit the dirt in front of the plate. One ball, one strike.

The next pitch looked great, like a fat balloon drifting toward him. Sylvester went into his swing, circling the bat around in a wide arc while simultaneously straightening his front leg.

Suddenly, a knife of pain stabbed at his ankle. He'd forgotten to put his ankle brace back on! He dropped the bat and hobbled out of the box.

"Sylvester, I thought you said your ankle was fine!" Coach Corbin's eyes were blazing with anger.

"It — it is," Syl stammered. "I just forgot my brace."

The coach gave him a long look. "Maybe I should tie a string around your finger so you'll remember," he said. "Take a seat. Rod Piper, you're up!"

Syl limped back to the bench, his face hot with embarrassment. He retrieved his brace and put it back on.

Burk retired the next two batters in ten pitches. Syl grabbed his glove and started for the outfield.

"Coddmyer!" the coach barked. "Stay on the bench and elevate that ankle. Piper, take his place in right field."

As Rod hurried onto the field, Coach Corbin handed Sylvester an ice pack. "Here, put this on that ankle. And remember your brace from now on!"

"Yes, sir," Sylvester whispered. He took the brace off again, stretched his left leg out on the plank beside him, and laid the pack on his ankle. Sitting like that made it impossible for anyone to sit next to him — not that that mattered, he soon found out, for no one seemed to want to go near him. No one even asked him how his ankle was feeling. When the teams switched sides, Trent and Kirk stood at the far end of the bench, even though Syl shifted to make room for them.

When practice finally ended, Sylvester felt like a complete outcast. Everyone else broke off into groups of twos or threes, laughing and talking about baseball. Sylvester dumped the now warm ice pack in the trash, put his brace back on, and trudged alone to the empty parking lot.

"Hey there, slugger!"

Syl's eyes widened. There was Charlie Comet, leaning against a tree! Syl was nearly positive the man hadn't been there a moment before. But the tree's branches were low and leafy, so maybe he just hadn't seen him.

"Tough day, huh?" Charlie said.

"I've had better," Syl admitted.

"You'll have better again, don't you worry." Charlie sounded so certain that Sylvester smiled.

"In fact," Charlie continued, "I'd be happy to work with you on your switch-hitting, if you're not too tired."

Sylvester snorted. "Tired? I've been warming the bench for the past hour! I'd love to —"

The toot of a car horn interrupted him. It was his mother, who had come to get him for his haircut.

"Rats, I gotta go," Syl said. Then an idea struck him. "Can we practice after dinner instead? My dad will be home then. He could join us."

"If that's what you'd like, sure," Charlie replied. "See you at the field later."

But when Sylvester suggested going to park for some practice that night, Mr. Coddmyer shook his head.

"Coach Corbin called while you were getting your haircut," he said. "Asked me if you were icing your ankle like he told you to."

Mrs. Coddmyer fixed a sharp eye on her son. "Sylvester! Did you hurt your ankle again and not tell me?"

71

"It's just a little, um, achy," Syl mumbled.

"Well, 'a little, um, achy' or not, you are not playing any more baseball today. And that's final!"

Sylvester thought about telling them that his new friend, Charlie, would be waiting for him at the park. But he wasn't sure how his parents would react to the news that yet another mysterious ballplayer had been working with him. He'd told them all about Mr. Baruth and Cheeko, but somehow, they'd never managed to meet either of those men.

In fact, something told Syl that even if he did convince his father to take him to the park, Charlie wouldn't show up. So in the end, he decided not to say anything.

12

The next day, Saturday, was bright and warm when Sylvester joined his parents at the table for breakfast.

"I'm going to pick up some things for our Fourth of July party next weekend," Mrs. Coddmyer announced. "Think you two can keep busy while I'm out?"

Mr. Coddmyer looked over his newspaper and gave Sylvester a wink. "Oh, I've got an idea or two of things we can do."

Mrs. Coddmyer raised her eyebrows but didn't say anything. She left soon after.

"So, Dad, what're your ideas?" Sylvester asked when they were alone.

His father ticked off his fingers. "We could clean the garage, weed the garden, wash the windows, or" — he smiled broadly — "we could head to the park and play baseball!"

"Yes!" Sylvester pumped his fist. "Thanks, Dad!"

"Why don't you call Duane or some of the other boys and see if they want to join us?"

Sylvester's enthusiasm faded. He wasn't sure his friends would accept the invitation, but he didn't feel like explaining why to his father. So instead he said, "Um, I'll see those guys at practice later today. How about we go to the batting cages? I've saved my allowance so I can pay my own way."

"A little father-son time it is. Go put on your brace. I'll get the gear and meet you in the car."

But when Sylvester returned a minute

later, his father wasn't in the car. He was staring at the bucket of balls.

"Where'd you get these?" Mr. Coddmyer asked curiously.

Syl bit his lip. This was the perfect opportunity to tell his father about Charlie Comet and the switch-hitting. But he hesitated — and then the phone rang.

"I'll get it!" Syl rushed inside.

"Coddmyer, Coach Corbin here," a voice boomed over the line. "We have our first game the morning of the Fourth of July. Some kids will be away for the holiday. Can you make it?"

"Sure, Coach," Syl assured him. "See you at practice." He hung up and returned to the garage. To his relief, his father was waiting for him in the car. He seemed to have forgotten about the baseballs.

When they arrived at the batting cages, Sylvester paid the attendant and got tokens for the pitching machines. He and his father selected bats and helmets and headed into the cages. Syl chose the slow-pitch option and took up a lefty stance.

"What th —?" Mr. Coddmyer said, sounding perplexed. "Did you become left-handed overnight?"

Syl hesitated. Once again, he had the chance to tell his father about Charlie. And once again, he decided not to.

Instead, he explained that batting righty made his ankle hurt.

"Just a bit!" he added hurriedly when his father frowned. "But I'm also trying lefty because I, um, heard that switch-hitters are good for a team."

At that, Mr. Coddmyer nodded. "True," he said. "There have been many great professional ballplayers who were switch-hitters. There's Pete Rose, Roberto Alomar, Chipper

76

Jones, and of course, the most famous switch-hitter of all, Mickey Mantle." His eyes twinkled. "Your grandfather, Sylvester Coddmyer the First, once played against Mantle, did you know that?"

Sylvester's jaw dropped. "What! No way!"

His father laughed. "Yes way."

"No, you're pulling my leg. Grandpa Syl never played in the pros!"

"Maybe not, but he did face Mantle once, when the Mick played for the Baxter Springs Whiz Kids in Oklahoma. That was back in the late 1940s, when they were both teenagers, before the Mick was drafted by the Yankees. Grandpa Syl claimed that he knew even then that Mantle was going to be a star. 'He was a big fella, muscular and blond, and could wallop the ball a mile on a clear day.' That's how he always started off his story about his brush with fame."

Mr. Coddmyer smiled at the memory. "You could ask my dad anything about the Mick and he would know the answer."

Then the smile faded. "Dad was heartbroken when it came out that his hero had a lifelong drinking problem. Mantle himself seemed pretty heartbroken when he realized he'd failed to be a good role model to young players like you. He tried to make up for it, though. Spent much of the last few years of his life teaching people about the dangers of alcohol abuse."

His father took a few swings with his bat. "You know, after your grandfather died, I found a stash of old photos from his Oklahoma baseball days in his belongings. We should look through them sometime. Maybe we'll spot a young Mickey Mantle!"

"Sure, that sounds great!" Syl replied. Then he took up his lefty stance again and pushed the start button on the machine. He tried hard to concentrate on the incoming ball, but his mind kept turning over what his father had said. He was interested in the fact that his grandfather had once played against Mantle. But it was the description of Mantle himself that really intrigued him.

Mantle had been big and blond. He was a switch-hitter. He could wallop the ball a mile. And he was a New York Yankee.

Syl knew someone who fit that description to a T — Charlie Comet!

13

Sylvester and his father stayed at the batting cages for more than an hour. During that time, Syl worked on his left-handed batting. He whiffed a fair number of pitches. But he also hit several, a few of them hard enough to billow the netting behind the pitching machines.

Finally, Mr. Coddmyer said it was time to go home. Sylvester didn't mind. He was thirsty, and hoped they could dig out those old baseball photos.

But just as they finished putting their gear away, Mrs. Coddmyer returned from her errands. She needed help unloading the car. When they were through, there was only enough time for a quick lunch before practice.

Mr. Coddmyer volunteered to drive him. He was unusually quiet for the first minutes of the ride. When he did speak, his voice was overly casual.

"Sylvester, you sat out most of practice yesterday, right?"

"Yeah," Syl replied.

"So you couldn't have practiced switch-hitting then. Which makes me wonder" — Mr. Coddmyer maneuvered the car into the parking lot, shut off the motor, and faced his son — "when *did* you practice? Who taught you how? And who suggested you try hitting lefty in the first place? I know you didn't teach yourself. It's obvious that you've been coached by someone who knows what he's talking about. It's not Coach Corbin because he would have mentioned it when we spoke last night. So who?"

Sylvester stared down at his hands. He knew he couldn't keep Charlie a secret anymore, not when his father was asking him point-blank. So he spilled the whole story, from the time Charlie had helped him with his ankle to the meeting yesterday under the tree.

Mr. Coddmyer drummed the steering wheel with his fingers. "Okay, Syl. You know I'll want to meet him." He gave his son a serious look. "Let's be sure that meeting happens this time. Not like with that fellow Cheeko and the other man, Mr. Baruth."

Syl nodded.

"Off you go, then. Have a good practice and don't forget to wear your brace. Your mother will have your head if you do!"

Sylvester unbuckled his seat belt and opened the door. "Don't worry, Dad, I'll wear it. And I'll make sure you meet Charlie! I promise!"

But as he ran to the field, he wondered if he'd be able to keep that promise. Would Charlie be a no-show, like Cheeko, or just never around when his folks were, like Mr. Baruth?

Coach Corbin was calling for attention when Sylvester reached the diamond. Trent, Duane, and Kirk were sitting together. But when Duane looked at him with narrowed eyes, Sylvester swallowed hard and sat someplace else.

Coach Corbin boomed, "We have our first game this Saturday. Some of you will be away, celebrating the Fourth, but we'll have enough players to make a team. Here's the roster."

He consulted his clipboard. "Burk Riley on the mound. Eddie Exton at catcher. First base, A. C. Compton. Bus, you're at second, with Trent at short. For third base, Duane. Leon, right field. Center field . . ."

Sylvester wasn't sure, but he thought the coach hesitated for a moment before saying ". . . Coddmyer. Kirk, left field. When the rest of you return after the Fourth, we'll shift things around."

He put his clipboard away and clapped his hands. "Take your positions. Everyone else, line up to bat. Your teammates need lots of fielding practice today."

Sylvester and the others hustled onto the field.

"Here we go, Burk, send it right on past him!" Trent yelled. "Look alive, guys, ready for that ball!"

"No batter, no batter, no batter, no batter!" Duane chanted.

Syl thumped his fist into his glove but kept quiet.

Rick Wilson was up first. He had a surprisingly strong swing for a pitcher. Even so, he missed the first two pitches.

"Come on, we want some hits!" A. C. called from first base. "We need the —"

Pow! Rick clobbered the next pitch right at A. C. Then A. C. lifted his glove. The ball socked into it with a satisfying *pop*.

"Next!" A. C. joked as he threw the ball back to Burk.

Rod Piper approached the plate. Burk zipped in three pitches for two strikes and one foul. Rod connected for a blooper over the mound on the fourth pitch. The ball bounced toward shortstop. Trent charged forward, scooped it up, and tossed the ball to A. C. for the out.

"Next!" A. C. repeated loudly. Everyone laughed.

Their laughter died quickly when the next

batter, a stocky boy named Stan Falls, blasted Burk's first pitch high in the air between left and center fields.

Syl immediately started running for it. So did Kirk.

"I've got it!" Kirk yelled as they neared the spot where the ball was dropping.

Syl slowed to avoid a collision. Suddenly, his foot caught on something in the grass. He pitched forward, arms out to break his fall.

"Oof!" He hit the turf at Kirk's feet. Kirk jumped to keep from stepping on him. Meanwhile, the ball fell out of the sky and — *plop!* — landed in Syl's outstretched glove.

Syl got up amidst scattered laughter. "Well, that catch has to be one for the record books!" he said, turning with a grin toward Kirk.

But Kirk wasn't grinning back. He was scowling. "Record books, huh? Is that all you think about, getting into the record books? Yeah, I'll bet it is." He spun away.

Sylvester stood stock-still. Any doubt he had had that Kirk knew about his cheap shot and dirty plays was completely gone. And in its place was another emotion: dread.

14

Sylvester felt sick. Kirk clearly thought he was a dishonest player, out for glory at any cost. And if he'd told Duane and Trent about his cheating, then they did, too.

I wish something would happen to end practice right now, he thought miserably.

Even as that thought crossed his mind, dark storm clouds appeared overhead. Ten minutes later, the sky opened up and unleashed a torrent of rain. Most of the Hawks took cover in the dugout, but Syl dashed across the field toward home. Somehow, he didn't think he'd be welcome in the dugout.

Syl slowed his pace when he spotted a bench. He sat down, took off his baseball cap, and leaned forward onto his elbows. Rain dripped through his hair and down his nose, but he was so deep in thought he barely noticed.

If I could just go back in time, I'd never listen to that rotten Cheeko's advice. Maybe I wouldn't have played that great last season, but at least the guys wouldn't hate me.

Suddenly, it stopped raining on him. He looked up. Charlie was standing behind him with a big black umbrella. "Thought you could use this. You looked like a drowned rat," the blond man joked. "Trouble at practice?"

Syl was too downhearted to even wonder how Charlie knew about that. "Yeah. And it's my own fault."

Charlie raised his eyebrows.

"I — I have a secret," Syl confessed.

"What kind of secret?" Charlie prodded.

"A bad one," Sylvester admitted. "Last baseball season, I got away with something — actually, a lot of somethings — that now I wish I hadn't." He told Charlie about Cheeko. "And because I was stupid enough to follow his advice," he finished, "Duane and my teammates think I'm a cheat. Which I guess I am." He leaned forward on his elbows again and hung his head.

Charlie blew out a breath. "I know all about Cheeko."

Syl looked up, surprised.

"And I know all about bad secrets, too." Charlie stared off into the distance. "I used to do something I didn't want anyone else to know about. I told myself what I was doing wasn't that bad. But finally, I couldn't deny my secret anymore." He turned his gaze back to Syl. "Owning up to the truth was one of the hardest things I've ever done. But you know what? Once my secret was out, I felt relieved."

"You did?"

Charlie nodded. "People weren't happy when they found out. Some felt betrayed. But lots understood and forgave me. And that gave me strength to move forward to make things right, instead of looking back and wishing things had been different."

Sylvester sighed deeply. "I still wish I could change the past."

"There's an old saying," Charlie said. "It goes something like 'Give me the strength to change the things I can and the grace to accept the things I cannot.' Ever hear it?"

Syl raised and lowered his shoulders.

"We all have things we wish we could do differently," Charlie said. "But the past is passed. All we can do is try to make amends and do things right in the future."

Syl put his baseball cap back on and tugged at the brim. "Do you think I can make things right with Duane and the others?"

"Won't know until you try." Charlie handed Syl the umbrella. "Here, take this. I'll be okay without it."

"Thanks," Syl replied. He started to leave. Then he looked back.

"Is there something else, Syl?"

It was on the tip of his tongue to ask Charlie if the name "Mickey Mantle" meant anything to him. But Syl swallowed the question without asking it. After all, what would he do if Charlie answered yes?

So instead he shook his head, waved goodbye, and set off for the fields. Earlier he'd avoided Duane, Trent, and Kirk. Now he wanted to find them, because he had something very important to tell them.

15

As it turned out, the only teammate he found was Duane. He was huddled under the same tree Charlie had once stood under. When he saw Syl heading toward him, he frowned.

Syl's step faltered. Then he squared his shoulders and continued on.

"Hi," he said. "Want to share my umbrella?"

Duane shrugged but got under anyway.

"I've got to talk to you about something," Syl said.

"What?"

Duane's voice was steely, not at all the tone Syl was used to hearing from his friend. Once again, he faltered. But he didn't give up.

"You might already know what I want to tell you. At least, I'm pretty sure Kirk knows, and I think he told you."

"Oh yeah?"

"Yeah." Syl plunged right in. "Remember me telling you about Cheeko?"

"The guy who looked like Eddie Cicotte?"

Syl nodded. "Yeah, him. He gave me some advice last season. I know now it was bad advice, but back then, I took it. And when I did, I started cheating. More than what Kirk told you about that jab I took at Russ and the catch I didn't really make." He sighed. "I can't change what I did, but I want you to know that I'll never cheat again."

He waited for Duane to say something. But his friend was silent.

He still doesn't trust me. Syl's heart sank.

"Syl," Duane said finally, "Kirk never told me anything about Russ or a catch."

Sylvester was stunned. "He — he didn't? Then why have you been so mad at me?"

Duane grimaced. "Because you have another secret you're not telling me, that's why."

"No, I —" Syl started to protest.

Then Duane opened his glove and removed an old baseball — the ball Syl had missed after Duke had dumped over the bucket. Syl snapped his mouth closed.

"Thought so," Duane said. "I'm outta here. Have fun playing with C. C., whoever he is."

"C. C.?" *Charlie Comet?* Sylvester grabbed Duane's arm. "Where'd you come up with those initials?"

Duane thrust the baseball into Syl's hand. "They're right here!"

Syl found the writing. His eyes widened. There were two letters, and each had a downstroke that then curved up and around to form what looked like a *C*. But there was also a second, smaller curve, like a hump attached to the top of each *C*, making the letters look like . . . *M*s!

"Tell me the truth, Syl," Duane spat angrily. "That day in the park? You pretended your ankle hurt just to get rid of me so you could play ball with whoever C. C. is! Some friend you are!"

Syl's jaw dropped. "What?! You don't really believe that, do you?"

Duane didn't answer. The only sound was the patter of rain on the leaves and the umbrella.

"Duane," Syl said at last, "you're my best friend. I would never want to get rid of you." He took a deep breath. "Can I explain about that day? Please?"

"Fine," Duane replied gruffly.

So Syl began talking, telling Duane how Charlie Comet had appeared right after he'd hurt his ankle, how he'd promised to help him get his game back on, and how he'd shown him to bat lefty.

As he explained, a look of understanding grew on Duane's face. "Another mystery man," he murmured. "Why didn't you tell me before?"

Sylvester dug his toe into the wet grass. "You would have thought I was crazy."

"Oh." Then Duane started laughing. Syl looked up, suddenly hopeful.

"Guess what? I already thought you were crazy!" Duane said. "And you know what would be even crazier? *Not* batting lefty, if it helps your batting *and* keeps your ankle from hurting!"

He stuck his hand out from under the umbrella. "Hey, it's stopped raining!" He poked Sylvester in the ribs good-naturedly. "Feel like playing some ball? I'll find Trent and Kirk and some others. I'll bet they're itching to get in some more practice, too. Especially Kirk. He can't stand Duke Farrell and is dying to beat the Grizzlies on Saturday. And who knows? Maybe together we can make you into a switch-hitter by then!"

Syl nodded happily and Duane took off to find their friends. Syl started to lower the umbrella. A movement in the bleachers caught his eyes. It was Charlie. He took off his New York Yankees cap, waved, and then hopped off the stands and disappeared into the trees behind them.

"Bye, Charlie," Sylvester murmured. "And thanks."

16

It didn't take long for Duane to round up some more Hawks. Trent and Kirk seemed surprised that Duane and Syl were friends again, but Duane took them aside and explained that everything was cool. After that, the four boys and the three other Hawks they tracked down set to work on their game.

The first time Sylvester took up his lefty stance, his teammates peppered him with questions about it. Duane stopped them by pointing out that batting lefty didn't hurt Syl's ankle. "And since we all know how good a batter Syl can be when he's in top form, I think we should help him be the best lefty he can be!"

The others shouted their agreement. No one questioned him any further — much to Syl's relief.

The diamond was muddy because of the rain, but the seven boys were having too much fun to care that their clothes were getting covered with dirt. The only thing Syl kept clean was the baseball Duane had given him. He thought he might do a little research on those initials when he got home.

But the next morning, the baseball was nowhere to be found.

Sylvester did locate something else he was interested in, however — the old photos of his grandfather. He and his father looked at them together at the kitchen table. Syl picked up a posed shot of his grandfather and stared at it.

"I always knew you looked like Grandpa

Syl," Mr. Coddmyer said. "You've got the same nose, eyes, and chin!"

"Think I got my love of baseball from him, too?" Syl asked.

"Maybe," his father replied. "Want to keep that photo?"

Syl nodded and then put the photo aside to look at the next. This was an action shot, taken from behind home plate during a game. Number 12, his grandfather, was chasing down a fly ball. The runner, meanwhile, was hotfooting it to first. Syl couldn't see the runner's face, but he could make out the team name on the back of the uniform.

Baxter Springs Whiz Kids, it read.

Syl's heart beat faster. Mickey Mantle's old team! He quickly riffled through the rest of the photos, hoping to find a clear shot of that runner or his teammates.

But the photographer had obviously been interested only in Sylvester Coddmyer the

First, not the Whiz Kids. Syl found out why when he saw a note the photographer had written on the back.

Taken by Julia West, April 14, 1947. Sylvester grinned. Julia was his grandmother, Grandpa Syl's wife. No chance she'd have taken photos of an unknown player on the other team, not when the love of her life was on the field!

Syl tucked that photo with the others back into their box and then put the box and the posed shot of his grandfather in his room. Then he set off for the baseball fields.

Sylvester had told his friends that he didn't want to test out his lefty batting abilities in front of the coach, at least not yet.

"I'm not ready," he insisted, and so they had agreed to keep mum. They had also agreed to meet him back at the field after dinner. It turned out they all wanted to get some extra practice so they could beat the Grizzlies on Independence Day.

Thanks to all the extra practice, Sylvester's lefty swing improved. His ankle, too, was scarcely bothering him anymore and he could bat righty without pain. Still, he didn't want to give up on becoming a switch-hitter. He remembered how Charlie had said he had gone far in baseball in part because he could bat both right and left.

Maybe someday, Syl thought, *I'll follow in his footsteps.*

The Fourth of July game was scheduled for ten o'clock. Sylvester and his parents arrived at nine-thirty for warmups. Syl was dressed in his new maroon-and-white uniform, with the word *Hawks* emblazoned across the chest. On the back was the number 12. He'd chosen it in honor of his grandfather.

The Grizzlies were warming up on an adjoining field. Sylvester wondered if Duke Farrell was there. *Maybe he's away for the holiday,* he thought.

But Duke was on the mound, hurling pitches as hard and as fast as ever. Syl remembered how one of those pitches had hit him last season — and remembered how Duke had promised to get even with him when they next met.

He quickly pushed both memories out of his head.

The umpire blew his whistle at ten o'clock sharp. The Grizzlies were up first, so the Hawks took to the field.

Sylvester thumped his fist into his glove as the first Grizzly batter came to the plate. "Here we go, Burk, here we go!" he yelled. "One-two-three, one-two-three!"

Burk Riley wound up and threw. The ball

zoomed on a line and socked into Eddie's glove.

"Strike one!" the umpire called. The Hawks fans cheered.

Burk got the ball back from Eddie, stared down the batter, and threw again.

Pow! The batter connected and the ball bounced through the infield grass toward third. Duane scooped it up and fired it at A. C. Compton at first. Toe on the bag, A. C. caught it moments before the runner tagged the base.

"Out!" shouted the umpire. The fans whistled and clapped.

Steve Button was up next. Steve was a blow-hard, but he was also a powerful hitter. Sure enough, he clobbered Burk's third pitch. The ball soared high in the sky, heading to a spot between center and left field.

"Take it, Syl!" Kirk cried.

Sylvester put on a burst of speed, stuck out his glove, and nabbed the ball before it hit the ground.

"Out!" the umpire called. Syl grinned and threw the ball back to Burk.

"Only one more!" Duane cried.

But the next batter laced a sizzling grounder between first and second for a single. Then Duke strode to the plate. He knocked the dirt from his cleats, adjusted his helmet, and stepped into the batter's box, twirling the bat in small circles over his shoulder while he waited for the first pitch.

Burk blazed one in, but it was too far outside.

"Ball one!"

The next pitch was also a ball. And the third was so close to Duke's midsection that he had to jump out of the way to avoid being hit. With the count 3 and 0, Duke naturally let the fourth pitch go by — and looked angry when the umpire called it a strike. On the next pitch, he seemed to take that anger out on the ball.

Crack! A deep blast to center field.

"I've got it!" Sylvester backpedaled and got under the ball. At least, he thought he got under it. At the last second, the sun blinded him and the ball fell behind him.

"Rats!" He spun, picked it up, and hurled it to Bus Riley at second. Too late! The runner was safe, and Duke stood on first with a smug smile.

"The throw is to any base!" Coach Corbin reminded his team.

But the Hawks didn't have to throw the Grizzlies out, for the fifth batter went down swinging.

"Start us off, Trent," the coach said. "Then it's A. C., Kirk, and Sylvester."

Sylvester's stomach did a flip-flop. Coach Corbin had put him in the clean-up spot. If

Trent, A. C., and Kirk all got on base, it would be up to him to hit them home.

But Trent didn't get on. Neither did A. C. Duke's pitches were so fast and hard they both struck out looking. That brought up Kirk. He lambasted his former teammate's first pitch down the third baseline. The third baseman missed the catch and by the time the Grizzly left fielder got the ball, Kirk was safe at second.

Now Syl walked to the plate. He got into a right-handed stance and waited.

Zip! Duke's first pitch blurred by him for strike one. So did the second.

Syl stepped out of the box and took a deep breath. Then he stepped back in, gripped the bat's handle, and stared down at Duke. *I'm going to hit this pitch if it's the last thing I do!*

Instead, the pitch hit him, right in the ribs!

"Take your base!" the umpire called. "And

Farrell, watch where you're putting that ball. I don't want any injuries today."

Duke nodded obediently, but Sylvester didn't miss the smirk on his face. He knew then that Duke had hit him on purpose. *Okay, now the score is even,* Syl thought.

I hope, he added silently.

Unfortunately, Eddie flied out to short to end the inning scoreless.

Neither team scored in the next two innings either. But in the top of the fourth, Steve Button slugged a homer over the left field fence. There was no way Kirk could have caught it, but still, he pounded his fist in his glove as if disgusted with himself.

Burk looked shaky after Steve's homer. He gave up a single to the next batter, and walked the one after that. Runners on first and second. No outs.

Luckily, Burk settled down and struck out two batters. Then the next one ground out to second and the dangerous scoring situation was defused.

Still, the score was 1–0 Grizzlies. The Hawks needed to get on the board.

They didn't. Duke gave up only one hit in the bottom of the fourth before retiring the side.

As Sylvester returned to the outfield, he thought about his own two at bats. Besides the first inning walk, he'd hit a foul ball that the third baseman had caught for an out. He knew he'd get up again the next inning. Maybe then he'd get a hit.

The Grizzlies started the top of the fifth with two hits to put runners on first and second. Then the third batter hit a grounder to short. Bus grabbed the ball and made a clean throw to Duane for the out. The next play was a duplicate of the one before it, with the same result. The nail-biter inning finally ended when a batter popped out to Burk.

In the dugout, Sylvester was checking to see when he'd be up when Snooky Malone called his name.

"Hey, Syl, you're doing good out there! Not like last season, but . . ." Snooky shrugged.

"Oh, Syl's got a few surprises up his sleeve, don't you worry!" Duane piped in. "Don't you, Syl?"

Syl blinked. Was Duane suggesting he should try batting lefty — against *Duke?* The idea terrified him. Then he realized it made sense. Duke was a right-handed pitcher, which meant a left-handed batter could give him trouble. Even better, he had no idea Syl could bat lefty.

The Hawks fans suddenly cheered. Kirk had just rapped out a single.

"Go get 'em, slugger," Duane said. And he handed Sylvester his favorite bat.

17

Sylvester walked to the plate. He'd decided he'd start off by batting righty. If he got on base, great. But if things looked bad, he'd switch to lefty and see what happened next.

Duke's first pitch came in low. Syl let it go by for a ball. The second one, a breaking ball, curved out at the last moment. Syl swung and missed. The count was 1 and 1.

Duke smirked as he caught the throw from his catcher. Syl suspected he was going to try the breaking ball again. He was right, but guessing what was coming didn't help him hit it. The umpire held up one finger on his left hand, two on his right.

Syl quickly stepped out of the batter's box and glanced over at Duane. Duane gave him the thumbs up, and then grabbed the coach's arm and started talking to him in a low voice.

The time had come. It was now or never. Sylvester crossed behind home plate to the box on the right and took up a lefty stance.

"Hey!" Duke cried from the mound. "He can't do that! Can he?"

The umpire held up a hand. "He left the box legally. Which side he hits from is up to him. Unless his coach . . ."

On the sideline, Coach Corbin simply nodded his approval.

Duke didn't argue further. Once again, he blazed in the same breaking ball. But this time, the pitch broke inward, toward Syl.

Like many batters, Syl found inside pitches

easier to hit than outside ones. This one was no exception.

Pow! The small white sphere disappeared into the clear blue sky, heading toward deep right. As the outfielder sprinted after it, Syl took off for first and Kirk hoofed it to second.

The ball bounced once. The fielder grabbed it and heaved with all his might toward first base.

Syl almost didn't beat the throw. But because he had bat lefty, he was one full step closer to first base. That one step was all he needed to make it there before the ball.

"Safe!" the first base umpire cried, fanning his arms out to either side.

The crowd roared. Coach Corbin pumped his fist. Duke looked angrier than ever. In fact, his next pitches were so wild that his coach finally had to pull him from the game. The Hawks lit up the new pitcher like a

Christmas tree. By the time the fifth inning ended, the score was 5–1. And when the Grizzlies couldn't score a man in the top of the sixth, the Hawks walked away with their first win.

"You did it, Syl!" Duane shouted. The Hawks surrounded Sylvester, cheering and laughing.

And Syl? He'd never been happier. That single had felt better to him than all the hits and homers he'd gotten the previous seasons, simply because he knew he had earned it through hard work.

Near the dugout, Snooky Malone was bouncing with such excitement that his glasses kept slipping down his nose. "That was so cool!" he said over and over.

Sylvester started laughing. "Thanks, Snook. By the way," he added casually, "does my horoscope say anything more about a comet?"

"No, it's no longer a factor in your future," Snooky informed him.

Sylvester smiled. "Yeah, that's what I thought. Oh well. It was nice while it was around." He threw an arm around Snooky's shoulders. "Come on. Everyone's meeting at my house for a Fourth of July party. Wouldn't be the same without my favorite sky watcher — or my best friend," he added, as Duane poked his head inside the dugout.

"What's taking you so long?" Duane cried. "We've got a celebration to go to!"

Epilogue

The rest of the summer season raced by. When it ended, the Hawks' record stood at 9 wins, 3 losses. Sylvester batted lefty in several games and got on base a few times. He made some good — but not spectacular — catches in the outfield, too. He looked for Charlie but never saw him again.

Not in real life, anyway.

The last weekend of summer vacation, the Coddmyers took a trip to Cooperstown, New York, to visit the Baseball Hall of Fame. There, Syl and his parents walked among exhibits of the greatest players the world has ever known. Syl spent a long time in an area dedicated to Babe Ruth. He didn't bother looking for Eddie Cicotte. He knew that player wouldn't be there.

In the Hall of Fame gallery, he glanced at several of the bronze plaques of the Hall's inductees. They were all interesting, but only one stopped him dead in his tracks.

As Syl stood there, staring at the face on the plaque, a member of the museum staff came up behind him.

"Mickey Charles Mantle," the woman said. "He's a favorite among visitors. The Mick, or the Commerce Comet, as he was sometimes known, was —"

Syl wheeled around. "Excuse me? What was that you called him?"

The woman looked surprised. "The Mick?"

"No, the other name."

"The Commerce Comet?"

Syl faced the plaque again. "Yeah," he said

softly. "Comet. That's it." He traced a finger over Mantle's middle name: Charles. "Thank you."

"You're welcome," the woman replied. She moved off to another part of the gallery, not realizing that Sylvester Coddmyer the Third had really been thanking someone else.

The #1
Sports Series
for Kids

Matt Christopher®

Read them all!

*Previously published as Crackerjack Halfback

All available in paperback from Little, Brown and Company

**Previously published as Pressure Play

Matt Christopher®

Sports Bio Bookshelf

Muhammad Ali

Lance Armstrong

Kobe Bryant

Jennifer Capriati

Jeff Gordon

Ken Griffey Jr.

Mia Hamm

Tony Hawk

Ichiro

Derek Jeter

Randy Johnson

Michael Jordan

Mario Lemieux

Tara Lipinski

Mark McGwire

Yao Ming

Shaquille O'Neal

Jackie Robinson

Alex Rodriguez

Babe Ruth

Curt Schilling

Sammy Sosa

Venus and Serena Williams

Tiger Woods